T0197610

Looney the Buck Tooth Chick

Barbara Hughes

illustrated by
Sienna Gordon and Percy Gordon iii

To order additional copies of this book, contact:
Xlibris
1-888-795-4274
www.Xlibris.com
Orders@Xlibris.com

Dedicated to my grandchildren,

Sienna, Percy, and Amber

Introduction

Barbara N. Hughes teamed up with her grandchildren to bring Looney to life. The two youngest grandchildren, Sienna Layla Gordon and Percy Gordon III, did the art. Amber Gordon assisted with book layout. Together they made a great team!

Planet Duckville is a beautiful planet that is full of interesting animals. The ruler of all these alien animals is King Duffey the Duck.

Before the baby ducklings could hatch, all their eggs had to be sent to a nearby planet, Planet Earth. The ducklings would break out of their eggs and then return to their home planet.

Among the duckling chicks was Prince Looney, the only chick born with a bucktooth. The bucktooth was a sign of royalty.

King Duffey awaited his son's arrival with great excitement.

As Looney sat in his spaceship, he heard a loud thump. Down went the ship with Looney hanging on for dear life!

Looney found himself among some strange-looking birds. They were making funny sounds. He wondered where such creatures came from, and if they were dangerous.

A cry went out all over Planet Duckville that Prince Looney's ship had gone down. Within minutes the sky filled with spaceships, so many that they turned the sky black.

Frightened for his son, the king instructed Earth's animals to help Looney in any way they could.

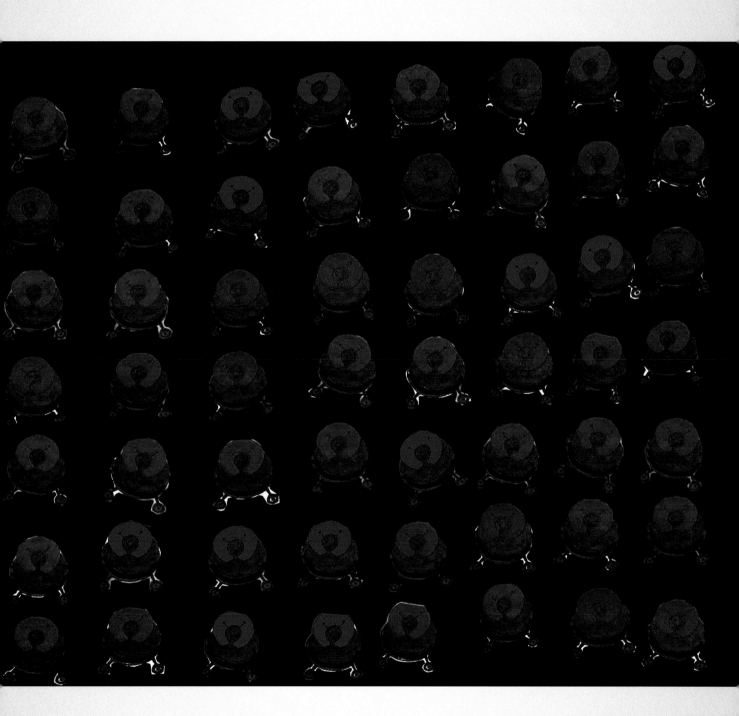

Looney knew that this was not home when he saw a strange creature walking toward him on two legs. Lucky for Looney, three other creatures appeared and kept the other two-legged creatures back, giving Looney a chance to get away. He ran and ran, wondering what to do.

Every animal of Planet Duckville is born with the ability to create a double image of itself to confuse attackers, so they can get to safety. Most animals learn from their parents. As Looney ran, he tried to figure out how to do it on his own.

Looney was so scared that he finally threw off a double image of himself. Success! He hoped that if the two-legged creature was following him, it wouldn't know which chick to attack.

Meanwhile, all of Planet Earth's animals were looking for Prince Looney. Shy Shy the Fox found Looney's footprints, and Alie the Alligator, Turf the Turtle, Thumper the Rabbit, and Duck Duck followed. They shouted Looney's name.

Shane the Bird and Lightning the Lighting Bug scouted from above, and made sure no one was following them that would endanger the prince. Soon they found Looney on a path, and told King Duffey where to land the royal spaceship.

At the end of the path, Looney saw his father waiting, and he knew that everything would be okay. They set out in the sunset and flew home in the royal spaceship.

THE END

Printed in the United States
By Bookmasters